LOLA LEVINE

and the

Vacation Dream

MONICA BROWN

LOLA LEVINE

and the

Vacation Dream

ILLUSTRATED BY
Angela Dominguez

LITTLE, BROWN AND COMPANY
New York • Boston

Text copyright © 2017 by Monica Brown
Interior Artwork copyright © 2017 by Angela Dominguez
Llama by Jinhwan Kim
Excerpt from *Lola Levine and the Halloween Scream*
copyright © 2017 by Monica Brown

Cover art © 2017 by Angela Dominguez. Cover design by Marcie Lawrence.
Cover copyright © 2017 by Hachette Book Group, Inc.

Little, Brown and Company

Hachette Book Group
1290 Avenue of the Americas, New York, NY 10104
Visit us at lb-kids.com

First Edition: April 2017

Little, Brown and Company is a division of Hachette Book Group, Inc.
The Little, Brown name and logo are trademarks of Hachette Book Group, Inc.

The publisher is not responsible for websites (or their content) that are not owned by the publisher.

ISBNs: 978-0-316-50639-7 (hardcover), 978-0-316-50638-0 (pbk.),
978-0-316-50635-9 (ebook)

Printed in the United States of America

LSC-C

10 9 8 7 6 5 4 3 2 1

For my mother,
Isabel Maria,
and my daughters,
Isabella and Juliana,
with love

CONTENTS

Chapter Five

Pachacamac.....62

Chapter Six

Flying Away.....73

Chapter Seven

Home.....82

Dear *Diario,*

Guess what? Tonight we all went to the opening of Dad's art show at a fancy gallery in the city. I didn't eat too many of the little cakes and sandwiches, even though they were tiny and I was hungry. I didn't jump or yell or bring my soccer ball, even though the show lasted for so many hours that I felt like jumping and yelling and kicking my soccer ball. Even Ben behaved, and he had to wear fancy clothes. Dad wore a black turtleneck and put his hair into a very nice ponytail, and Mom wore red, of course. I didn't realize how many people know my dad

and his paintings. Ben and I stayed
by Mom, but I snuck up to Dad for
a hug a couple of times because
I wanted everyone to know that I,
Lola Levine, am his daughter. Dad
was super happy afterward, and
on the long drive home Mom, Dad,
Ben, and I sang songs in English,
Spanish, and sometimes both!

Shalom,
Lola Levine

Chapter One
Flying High

I wake up the next morning with my dog curled up at the foot of my bed. I'm so glad it's Saturday!

"Good morning, Bean. Did you sleep

well?" I ask. Then I notice there is a note on Mia's goldfish bowl.

"Family meeting today!" it says. "The usual time and place."

I'm excited, because Mom and Dad only have family meetings when they have something big and fun to tell us. The usual time and place is our kitchen table during breakfast.

"Good morning, sunshine girl!" Mom says. "Did you get my note?"

"Yes! Yay! What's the surprise?" I ask.

"We need to wait for Ben to come down," says Mom.

"Hi, Lola!" says Dad, and kisses the top of my head. He's making scrambled eggs. Mom is making a big fruit salad.

"Yum!" I tell her. "Can I help?"

"Sure," says Mom. "You can cut up the mangos if you are very careful." Mom helps me cut them up.

"Mangos are my favorite," I say.

"You know—" my mom starts to speak.

"I know, I know," I say. "Mangos are much sweeter in Peru. You've told me! But I was only three the last time I was there, so I can't remember. I do remember Tía Lola taking me to the park every day, though."

"That's too bad," says Dad, "because, really, there's nothing as delicious as a Peruvian mango."

I take the fruit salad to the table, and Mom pours us all warm milk with sugar and just a splash of coffee—a special weekend treat. Just then I hear a loud *thwunk*, which is my brother, Ben, jumping down the last three stairs.

"Ben," I say, shaking my head, "you couldn't sneak up on anyone if you tried."

"Family meeting! Family meeting!" he yells, ignoring me. At least I think he's ignoring me, until he jumps on my back and says, "Boo!"

I don't think before I spin around fast and send Ben zooming into the air and onto the table. The fruit salad goes flying. What a mess.

"Are you ready for our family meeting?" Dad asks when we finally finish cleaning up the fruit.

"Yes!" Ben and I say at the same time.

"Well," says Mom, "last night, Dad sold lots of his paintings."

"That's because they are so awesome!" I say.

"Thanks, honey," Dad says, smiling.

"This means we will have extra money this month, and Dad and I have been talking about how to use it."

"I know!" says Ben. "Let's buy another puppy! Or a rocket ship…"

"I think we have our hands full with Bean," Dad says, "but what we are thinking does involve flying."

"A trip? Where?" I ask, crossing my fingers. There's only one place I want to go and one person I want to see. I look at Mom hopefully. I haven't seen my aunt Lola in almost two years. I'm named after her. I was in kindergarten when she came for my mom's thirtieth birthday.

Tía Lola is a couple of years younger than Mom, and she is fun and awesome. I write her letters all the time and she writes back. We also talk on the phone on weekends.

"Well," Mom says, "we were actually thinking we could visit Tía Lola in Peru."

"Really truly?" I ask Mom.

"Really truly," she says, and I can see that she's just as happy as me.

"Tía Lola still lives in the same house we both grew up in, but she rents rooms to an older woman and her daughter, a nurse. Lucky for us, they are both going to visit family in the north in a few weeks, so there will be room for all of us," Mom says. "You and Ben can sleep in the room I had when I was your age!"

"That would be so cool," I say.

"I have a very important question," says Ben. "Can we bring Bean?"

"Definitely not," says Dad. "The flight would be too long for him. We'll find someone nice for him to stay with."

"Are we taking an airplane to Peru?" Ben asks.

"Of course!" I say. "That's the only way to get there."

"You can't go by rocket ship?" Ben asks.

"Only astronauts fly in rocket ships," I say. "Tía Lola lives in Lima, which is the capital of Peru, by the way. It's on another continent, not outer space!"

"Don't be such a know-it-all," Ben says, and sticks out his tongue.

"Mom says that being a know-it-all

is just fine. It just means that I study a lot."

"Then you're a show-off!" Ben says.

"Well, I'm showing off all that I know," I say back.

"Hey! Let's be kind to one another," says Dad, but he's looking at me.

"I know," I tell Ben. "When we go to the library this afternoon, we can get some books about Peru."

"And then you two can read them together," says Mom.

"Yay!" says Ben. "Then I can show Tía Lola that I'm a know-it-all, too."

"For now," Dad says, "do you two want to look at Peru on a map?"

"Yes!" we say, and we all go to the computer.

Later in the week, Mom sets up an appointment with my teacher, Ms. Garcia. We are going to Peru for ten days, and I'm going to miss a whole week of school. We need to talk about it because I am in second grade and that's an important grade.

"I am excited for you, Lola," says Ms. Garcia. "This will be a great learning opportunity, so don't worry about missing school."

"I'll get to speak Spanish all day," I say, "and go to school with my *tía* Lola. She's a teacher like you, except now she's a principal, too!"

"That's great," says Ms. Garcia.

"What can Lola do to make up some of the work she will miss?" Mom asks.

Ms. Garcia thinks about it and says, "Lola, why don't you write a couple of short reports about Peru while you are there, and when you get back you can present them to the class."

"I like that idea," I say, because I love to write. Ms. Garcia knows this. "What about?"

"I'll let you choose," says Ms. Garcia, smiling. "You always have lots of ideas. I'll also give you a few math worksheets."

Mom and Ms. Garcia talk a little longer—in Spanish, as usual. Luckily, I understand everything they are saying. One of my super best friends, Bella Benitez, is Mexican American, and sometimes we speak Spanish to confuse our other friends, Josh Blot and Juan Gomez, who don't understand. They think we are saying secret girl-stuff, but usually we are just being silly and saying things like, *"El cielo es azul,"* which means, "The sky is blue."

Chapter Two
The Two Lolas

Dear Tía Lola,

Guess what?! I am writing to you from an airplane. We are on our way to see you! I'm so excited.

It's been a fun flight. The flight attendant gave me earphones, and I'm listening to music. I finished my math worksheets already because I'm so good at math. Dad is sleeping, and Mom is trying to keep Ben busy so he doesn't think about throwing up. He was doing fine until there were a few bumps and the plane shook. Then he said his stomach hurt, and we all know what that means. I like it when the plane moves up and down, because it feels like a roller coaster and I love roller coasters. Dad said that I probably shouldn't yell "Woo-hoo!" every time the plane bounces, but Ben was louder than me. He was moaning so loudly that the lady in front of him turned around to see what was wrong. I told her not to worry, that we Levines are just loud people. Then Ben started to gag and she turned back around real fast! Mom wants me to try to sleep, but how can I do that when I'm on my way to see my favorite aunt in the whole wide world?

Shalom,
Lola Levine

I do finally fall asleep and only wake up when the pilot announces that we are landing. Since I'm by the window, I get to see the lights of Lima, Peru. It's dark out, so they sparkle everywhere! It looks like a fairyland.

"Think about it, kids," Dad says. "Each light represents a house full of people, or a restaurant, or a store...."

"There must be a lot of people in Lima," I say, and wonder which light is my *tía* Lola's.

After we get off the plane, we get our luggage, stand in a long line, and show our passports to official-looking people. Then, finally, we are outside. I look everywhere but don't see a face that I recognize.

"Where's Tía Lola?" I ask Mom impatiently.

Then I hear a loud clear voice say, "Lola!" and I turn and there she is—my *tía* Lola. She looks a lot like my mom, except she has short hair just like me. She has big silver earrings and an even bigger smile on her face. I run to her and jump into her arms.

"You smell like Tía Lola!" I say. "And like Peru." Tía Lola laughs and holds me tighter. When she finally lets me go, Mom, Dad, and Ben take their turns.

"Lo!" Mom says, and she and Tía Lola hug and jump up and down. They both start crying.

"Don't cry," says Ben, looking worried.

"Shhh. It's okay," I tell him. "They are happy tears."

"Is that something only girls do?"

"No!" I say, and point to Dad, who is wiping away a few tears, too.

"Benito!" Tía Lola says. "Lola! You've both grown as tall as the sky."

"I'm in kindergarten now," Ben says, "and I didn't throw up on the plane!"

"Good for you!" Tía Lola says, and tweaks his cheek.

"And I'm a second grader," I say, "and I'm still awesome at soccer!"

"Of course you are." Tía Lola winks. "Now let's get you home!"

We drive for a while until finally I see a big white cement sign that reads LINCE.

"This is our district!" Mom says, and asks Tía Lola to drive around the neighborhood.

"Is the Chinese market still on the corner, Lo?" Mom asks.

"Yes!" says Tía Lola. "Señor Chang's granddaughter runs it now."

"Why is there a Chinese market in Peru?" asks Ben.

"Peru has lots of people of many backgrounds—including Chinese Peruvians," she tells Ben.

"What kind of Peruvian am I?" I ask Tía Lola.

"Well," says Tía Lola, "you are Spanish and indigenous Peruvian."

"And Peruvian American," adds Dad.

"And that's just on my side of the family," says Mom. "My darling, you are a citizen of the world!" Then she points out the window. "Oh, look! That's the place your *tía* and I would go get *butifarras* on weekends."

"What are *butifarras*?" asks Ben.

"They are a type of sandwich with *jámon del país*, country ham. They have red onions and chilies, too," Tía Lola explains.

"Is country ham different from city ham?" Ben asks.

"Good question, Ben," answers Tía Lola. "I don't know."

"Look, that's the very same movie theater I used to go to," says Mom.

"I still go there," says Tía Lola.

"Our house is on Avenida Julio C. Tello," Mom says, pointing to a sign. "Julio C. Tello was an amazing archeologist. He discovered many ruins in Peru that helped Peruvians learn more about our past."

"He was also the first indigenous archeologist," says Tía Lola. "Our students learn about him."

"What does 'indigenous' mean?" asks Ben.

"'Indigenous' refers to the first peoples

in Peru—the original peoples native to this land. Some of our ancestors are indigenous and others are Spanish."

"Do you like being a teacher, Tía Lola?" I ask.

"I love it," she says. "Though now that I'm the principal, I don't have just one class—I'm responsible for every student in the school. I hope you and Ben can come with me this week."

"That would be awesome," I say, and I mean it. But then I think of some of the problems I've had at my own school with kids teasing me. "Do you think they'll like me?" I ask.

"I don't think they'll like you, Lola—I think they'll love you!" Tía Lola says, and blows me a kiss from the front seat. I love my *tía* Lola so much.

"There are many things we could do in Peru, but you are here for such a short time!" Tía Lola says.

"I know," says Mom, "but I could only get a little time off work, and the kids have school. We didn't want to wait until next summer to see you, Lo. What matters most is that we are together."

"I agree," says Dad.

"Besides," Tía Lola says, "you can see ancient ruins right here in the city."

"I want to see ruins!" Ben yells. Then he pauses. "What are ruins?"

"They're the buildings and temples created by the first peoples in Peru, before the Spanish came. The ruins are over a thousand years old. Some could have been made by our ancestors," Tía Lola says. "We'll visit them next weekend."

Mom talks to Tía Lola in Spanish for the rest of the car ride, which is fine by me, because I understand most of it.

"Here we are!" says Mom. "Kids, this is the house Lo and I grew up in!" I look and see a small orange and gray house made of cement. Across the street are apartment buildings.

We bring our luggage inside, and Tía Lola shows us where we will sleep.

"This was the room Lo and I shared

when we were little," Mom says. It has two beds.

Ben jumps on one of the beds and says, "I call this one!" Then he jumps from one bed to the other.

"Ben!" I say. "Don't break the beds!"

"It's okay," says Tía Lola with a wink. "Your mom and I used to do that all the time."

"See, Lola!" Ben says, sticking out his tongue. "It's okay."

We're at Tía Lola's house! Everything is better than okay.

Lola Levine
Ms. Garcia's class
Report #1

Julio César Tello

Julio C. Tello was born in the Andes Mountains of Peru and grew up speaking Quechua, an indigenous language. He became a famous archeologist. An archeologist is someone who studies humans from the past and looks at the things and buildings people left behind. They dig to uncover buildings buried by sand and dirt. Julio C. Tello made many discover-ies in the Andes. My mom and my aunt grew up on a street named after him!

Chapter Three
San Martín Elementary School

Dear *Diario*,

Tomorrow I'm going to a Peruvian elementary school with my aunt Lola. I can't believe she's the principal, because she's nothing like the principal of my school at home. Principal Blot is serious, and Tía Lola is always smiling. Principal Blot gets mad at me sometimes, and Tía Lola never does. But Principal Blot is a lot nicer when I go over to her house to play with her son, my super best friend Josh. Mom says that Tía Lola is one of the youngest principals ever, but she is so amazing that they put her in charge of the school!

Shalom,
Lola Levine

We have to wake up very early to get ready for school because it is on the other side of the city. Tía Lola makes *café con leche* different from Mom. Mom uses fresh milk, but Tía Lola uses evaporated milk, sugar, boiling water, and a teaspoon of instant coffee. After we eat an egg over rice and some delicious Peruvian mangos, Ben and I get into Tía Lola's bright red van and drive to la Escuela San Martín de Porres. Tía Lola drives super fast! But it seems like everyone else in Peru does, too.

"There are so many people!" Ben says, looking out the window.

"We have almost ten million people living in the city," says Tía Lola, honking at a car that cuts in front of her.

"How many zeros are in ten million?" asks Ben.

"Seven," I say.

"That's right," says Tía Lola.

"Know-it-all," Ben says from the backseat. "But I bet you don't know who San Martín is, do you?"

"No, I don't," I say, and give Ben a glare.

"He's a saint! He helped the sick and the poor," Ben says. "Tía Lola told me!"

"I guess I'm not the only know-it-all," I tell Ben, and he smiles.

When we finally get to the school, I'm a little surprised, because there isn't a big playground with grass. The school is set up sort of like a square, and in the middle of the square there's a big dirt field.

Tía Lola must be reading my mind because she says, "This isn't a rich school, and we only have running water for a half hour twice a day. We spend money on books, not grass. Don't worry, though. The kids play soccer out here at recess."

I think about my school with the big playground and the green field where we play soccer and tag. I want San Martín Elementary to have those things, too.

We walk into the building, and everyone says, *"Buenos días*, Directora Valdez." *Directora* means "principal" in Spanish. It always surprises me to remember that Tía Lola is Dolores Valdez. Valdez was my mom's last name before she married my dad. I once asked her if I had to change my name when I got married, and she smiled and said, "Only if you want to."

Tía Lola takes me into the second grade classroom and introduces me to the teacher, Mr. Sánchez.

"Welcome to class, Lola," he says in Spanish. "I'm Mr. Sánchez." He then waves me to come forward and introduces me to the rest of the class.

"This is Lola Levine. She is Directora Valdez's niece. Let's all welcome our new friend to San Martín," Mr. Sánchez tells the class. I'm surprised when the students start clapping and smiling at me.

One of the students says, "*Hola*, Lola!" and then everyone starts saying it. I like the way it sounds. One of the things that

I notice is that a lot of the students are wearing bright green sweat suits. They almost look like soccer warm-up suits. Others have on green sweaters.

"Why do they match?" I ask Tía Lola quietly.

"The students all wear uniforms at our school—they have formal uniforms and sweat suits," Tía Lola whispers. "And if students can't afford to buy them, we provide the uniforms for free. This way, everyone looks the same and nobody worries about what they wear." I think about the times I've been teased by Alyssa Goldstein and Makayla Miller for being different or weird, and I think uniforms might be okay, especially if they look like soccer warm-ups!

"Have a seat here between Lucia and Lucas," Mr. Sánchez says. I say good-bye to Tía Lola and walk over to the chair.

"Have a good morning!" Tía Lola says. "I'll see you at lunch." Then she takes Ben's hand and says, "Ready to meet the kindergartners?" He looks a little scared and doesn't say a word until Tía Lola winks at him and says, "Can you give me a super-strong Ben-style high five?" And that's exactly what he does.

I sit down, and it seems like the whole class is looking at me.

"Where are you from?" a girl asks in Spanish.

"The United States," I reply.

"I'm Lucas," the boy on the other side

of me says. "That is my sister, Lucia." They look a lot alike.

"Hi!" Lucia says. "We're twins."

"Wow, it must be fun to have a twin," I say.

"Most of the time," Lucia says. "Do you like soccer?"

"Do I like soccer?" I repeat, laughing. "I think it is the best game in the whole wide world."

Then both Lucas and Lucia say, "You can be on my team!" at the exact same time.

Mr. Sánchez calls the class to attention and starts talking about the math lesson. Mr. Sánchez talks really fast! I'm glad we are doing math first because numbers translate across languages—and schools—very well.

"Goooooooooooooooooooooooooooooal!" Lucas yells as our team scores. I'm on Lucas's team because they needed a goalie. Everyone is running and yelling and going for the ball, and it's super fun. We kick up dirt and dust in the middle of the square and nobody cares. Not everyone is playing soccer. Some kids are standing in a circle playing a hand clapping game and others are just running around yelling. At first I don't see Ben anywhere, but then I realize he's in one of the run-around-yelling groups. That's my brother.

Lucia takes a shot, but I stop the ball.

"Good try," I say.

"Not good enough," she says, and two minutes later, she scores against me. I don't think I've ever met a player as competitive as me. I wonder if she likes to write, too? After a while, Tía Lola finds us in the square and takes us to her office for lunch. I don't really want to leave my new friends, but I do want to see my *tía* Lola.

We are hot and dusty when we walk into the main office, and it's nice to feel a gust of cool air. There is an air-conditioning unit in the office, but nowhere else in the school. It wasn't too hot in the morning, but now that the sun is out, I wonder how hot the classrooms will be.

"Well, what do you think of our school?" Tía Lola asks us.

"It's amazing!" says Ben. "Listen! I can say my ABCs in Spanish now, after only one morning. Except it's called the *abecedario* here." Ben starts singing. He doesn't seem to want to stop, so Tía Lola and I start eating.

Lola Levine
Ms. Garcia's class
Report #2

Fútbol/Soccer

Fútbol (the Spanish word for "soccer") is the most popular sport in Peru and South America. The Peruvian national team is called la Blanquirroja, "the white and red," the colors of the Peruvian flag. The 1930s and the 1970s were the golden ages of Peruvian soccer because the team won a lot, but

I hope there is another golden age in the future. I want them to score lots of goooooooooooooooo ooooals!

Chapter Four
Llamas and *Lúcuma*

Dear *Diario*,

Today was my third day at la Escuela San Martín. I'm having so much fun! I made two super-cool friends named Lucia and Lucas, and we promised to become pen pals after I leave. Lucia doesn't like to write as much as I do, but Lucas does and he promises they will write notes that Tía Lola can include with her letters. At San Martín, history is my hardest subject. There is so much I don't know about Peru, even though it's the place my mother was born. I'm not even gone yet and I already want to come back.

Shalom,
Lola Levine

A few days later, Tía Lola takes an afternoon off and announces that we are all going to visit the artisan markets in the Miraflores neighborhood of Lima. We leave San Martín right after lunch.

"What's an artisan?" Ben asks.

"An artisan makes art and crafts by hand. Most of the crafts you will see today are made by indigenous people from the Andes Mountains."

"Who buys them?" I ask.

"We do," says Tía Lola, "and tourists do, too. They are very beautiful, as you will see."

We visit a place called the Mercado Indio, the Indian Market. I can't believe my eyes. It seems like there are hundreds of booths filled with treasures. I've never seen so many beautiful blankets, rugs, dolls, mirrors, dresses, bags, ceramics, jewelry, baskets, and paintings. I don't know if I have words for all the colors I see—royal blue, hot pink, gold, turquoise, red, and bright purple. There are stuffed llamas like the one I have at home and beautiful dolls. I also see *chullos*, which are hats made of wool that have flaps around the ears. I have one that Tía Lola sent me and wear it whenever it's cold.

"These are the colors of Peru," Mom says.

"I like the colors of Peru," I say.

"Me too!" says Ben, and then he's off and running. Mom and Dad follow him, but I stay with Tía Lola. We hold hands and walk through the market.

"I like the people of Peru, too," I say, squeezing her hand.

We walk through a maze of booths, and each one is cooler than the next. I think about my dad and his paintings. I'm glad there are so many different kinds of artists in the world.

We walk and look, and pretty soon we run into Mom, Dad, and Ben, who says, "Lola! Look! I got a stuffed llama! One for me and one for Mira! It's made of real llama wool!" Mira Goldstein is Ben's best friend. She's very nice, even though her sister, Alyssa, is not as nice, in my opinion.

"Let's get a gift for Ms. Garcia," Mom says. "Maybe we can get something for the classroom."

"Great idea," says Dad.

"Can I get gifts for Josh and Bella, too?" I ask.

"Of course," says Mom. I pick out some earrings for Bella, a Peru national soccer team shirt for Josh, and a little painting of a llama for Ms. Garcia.

Mom buys a big rug that she says she will hang on the wall.

"But, Mom," Ben says, "rugs go on the floor!"

"Not this one," says Mom. "It's too beautiful. I want to look at it, not walk on it."

"I'm hungry," Ben says.

"Me too," says Tía Lola. "Let's get a *lúcuma* ice cream!"

"Ice cream before dinner?" Ben asks.

"Why not?" says Tía Lola.

"I bet Mom and Dad won't let us," says Ben.

"I think we should follow Tía Lola's rules while we are in Peru," Mom says, laughing. "Besides, it's vacation!"

"No rules on vacation!" Ben says, jumping up and down.

"Well, maybe some," Dad says, looking a little worried. We walk until we find an ice-cream stand, and a few minutes later I'm licking a bright orange ice-cream cone. *Lúcuma* is a green fruit that grows on trees. It's yellow-orange on the inside, with a great big dark pit. I've never tried an actual *lúcuma*, only the ice cream, and I love it.

"Knock, knock," Ben says.

"Who's there?" Tía Lola asks.

"I scream!" Ben yells.

"I scream who?" Tía Lola shouts back.

"I scream for *lúcuma* ice cream!" says Ben.

When we finish our ice cream, Tía Lola takes us to Plaza Mayor, the main square in the center of Lima.

"It looks like we are surrounded by castles!" I say.

"We are." Tía Lola laughs, and she points out the Government Palace, the Archbishop's Palace, and the City Palace, which is painted bright yellow. There are flowers and fountains everywhere. I've never seen such beautiful buildings.

"These were built by the Spanish," Tía

Lola says. "On Saturday, we are taking you to see buildings a lot older than this, which were built by the first peoples of Peru."

"I can't wait," I say, and then notice that Ben is trying to climb into a fountain.

"Ben!" I say. "That's not allowed."

"But I'm so hot," he says, and before I know it, he's in the water.

"Mom! Dad!" I yell, and reach over to try to grab his hands.

"Ben!" Dad says.

"Stop, Lola!" Mom says. "We'll get him!"

But I've already got Ben's two hands. I pull, but Ben pulls harder.

Splash! I fall into the fountain. Now tourists are taking pictures of Ben and me. By the time we get out of the water, Mom and Dad aren't too happy with us.

"I was trying to help!" I say.

"Aren't I strong?" Ben says. "I pulled Lola in!"

"Well, at least everyone's cooled off!" Tía Lola says cheerfully. "I think it's time to go home and get dry."

And that's exactly what we do. It's funny to think that this week, "home" is Tía Lola's house. And Mom's house, too.

The next day, at San Martín Elementary, Tía Lola packs me a lunch so I can eat on the playground with Lucia and Lucas. I have chicken with rice, leftovers from our dinner the night before. It's so yummy.

"Guess what?" I tell them. "We are going to Pachacamac this weekend to see the ruins." "Pachacamac" is a very fun word to say. It sounds like *pa-cha-ka-mack*.

"That's great! We went there on a field trip last year," says Lucia.

"They have llamas that walk around the museum," says Lucas.

"I thought llamas lived in the mountains," I say.

"They do! My dad's family had them growing up," Lucas explains. "When he moved to Lima, he couldn't bring them. The tourists like to take pictures of llamas, though, so you can find them in some places."

"I'm not a tourist," I say. At least I don't think I am. "My mom was born here—just like my *tía* Lola, I mean Directora Valdez."

"So you are Peruvian and American?" Lucia says.

"Yep," I say, and we both smile.

"Soccer?" asks Lucas.

"Definitely!" I say, and off we go.

Lola Levine
Ms. Garcia's class
Report #3

Llamas

Llamas are amazing! They live with people in the Andes Mountains. They are very social and like to live in herds. They are in the camel family of animals and are vegetarians. They are very friendly, unless you make them mad. Then they will kick and spit. Llama hair can be used to make rugs, ropes, and clothes. Llamas are also very useful. They help carry heavy loads and guard sheep. Peruvians love and celebrate llamas, and I do, too!

Chapter Five
Pachacamac

Dear *Diario,*

Guess what? It's almost midnight! I don't think I've ever been awake this late. Ben and I got to stay up late because Tía Lola and Mom were telling stories from when they were little. I guess Tía Lola got in trouble sometimes, just like me. Today was my last day at San Martín. Lucia, Lucas, and I had the best soccer game ever! It was hard to say good-bye to them and all the other kids, but I promised my new friends that I would be back. I sure hope that's true. Tomorrow, Tía Lola is taking us to the ruins at Pachacamac. I'm going to sleep now so I have energy to climb pyramids tomorrow.

Shalom,
Lola Levine

We wake up and drive to Pacha-camac. Ben brings his stuffed llama, of course. Since he got it, he hasn't put it down once. He even brings the llama into the bathroom with him.

The ride seems to take forever, but that's just because I'm so excited. When we finally arrive, we go to the entrance to buy our tickets.

We walk through the gates, and Tía Lola says, "Before we walk to the ruins, we are going to meet the llamas." She takes us into a big yard with lots of green grass and plants near the museum. Then I see them.

"Llamas!" I say. They are beautiful. They have lots and lots of fluffy fur—white, brown, and beige.

"They spend a lot of time around people," a museum worker tells us.

"Are they happy?" I ask.

"These llamas are healthy and happy. They are very special to us. Would you like to pet one?"

"Yes," I say, and he brings a llama over to me.

"I'd like you to meet Lorenzo."

"Hi, Lorenzo the llama," says Ben.

"Nice to meet you!" I say, and I pet him. The fur feels soft and rough at the same time. Lorenzo is much taller than me and has brown and white fur.

"I want to pet the llama, too!" Ben says. "He looks like my llama but a lot bigger!"

"But remember, he's real, so be gentle," Dad says, and surprisingly, Ben is.

"I think it's time to say good-bye to the llamas," Mom says after a while. "There is so much more to see."

"Good-bye, llamas!" I say.

"I'm going to name my llama Lorenzo, too!" Ben says. "Say good-bye to Lorenzo... Lorenzo."

We walk toward the ruins of buildings and courtyards and pyramids that look like nothing I've ever seen before. Everything is the color of sand, maybe because we are near the ocean. There are so many places to see.

"Can you imagine our indigenous ancestors living here?" Tía Lola says.

"When did our ancestors stop living here?" I ask.

"Yeah, why don't people live here now?" Ben asks. "I think it's cool! There are so many places to climb and hide."

"It is a very complex history," says Mom.

"I'm complex," I say.

"That's true," she says, smiling at me. "There have been indigenous peoples

67

living in Peru for over eleven thousand years. But around five hundred years ago, Europeans from Spain came and wanted to conquer the indigenous peoples and take their gold and use their land."

"That's not nice!" says Ben.

"No, it isn't," says Tía Lola. "But even though many died, and the Spanish destroyed this temple and stole the gold, indigenous people are strong, and we found ways to survive. We're still here. Some are like us and have a mix of Spanish and indigenous backgrounds. But not all are mixed. There are many indigenous groups in Peru who speak their native languages and maintain their traditions." She hugged me close.

"We're smart and creative people," I say, and I feel proud that I am Peruvian.

"Here it is!" says Tía Lola. "The Temple of the Sun." We climb up the steps of the pyramid, and when we finally reach the top, I'm amazed. I see parts of the walls and imagine the courtyards and buildings filled with the first peoples of Peru. I see the blue ocean beyond.

"Guess what?" says Ben.

"What?" I say.

"I feel really close to the sun up here," he says.

"Guess what?" I say.

"What?" says Ben.

"I do, too."

Lola Levine
Ms. Garcia's class
Report #4

Pachacamac

Pachacamac is an archeological site that was named after the creator god Pacha Kamaq. The Temple of the Sun, the Painted Temple, and the Old Temple of Pachacamac can be found here. The first indigenous peoples to live at Pachacamac were the Lima people over a thousand years ago, and the last were the Inca people, who came around 1450. Archeologists like Julio C. Tello helped uncover these cultures.

Chapter Six

Flying Away

Dear Grandma Levine,

Hi, Bubbe! Guess what?! I'm writing to you from another continent, South America. Actually, I'm writing to you from my mom's old desk in her old house in

Lima, Peru. Isn't that neat? I love it here and I am learning a lot! How are you? When are you going to visit? How are the friends you play cards with? Someday we should go to Peru together. I know you would love it as much as I do.

Shalom,

Lola Levine

Tía Lola throws a big party for us all before we leave. She and Mom make all our favorite Peruvian foods. A lot of cousins and friends of my mom come to the party, and I meet some family members for the very first time! I don't think I realized just what a big family we have in Peru. I can tell Mom has had fun catching up with everyone this week while Ben and

I were at school with Tía Lola. Eventually, Tía Lola turns on music, and everyone starts dancing.

"Louder!" says Mom, who is dancing with Dad. I can't believe what a good dancer my mom is.

"We need to have more dance parties when we are back in the USA!" I yell over the music.

"Definitely!" Mom says, and then she grabs my hands and swings me around and around and around.

The next morning, before we leave, Tía Lola asks if I want to take a walk. First

we walk to the corner store, and she buys me some Peruvian candy and treats for the plane. Then we get *lúcuma* ice-cream cones and walk to the park. I'm feeling sad about leaving, and I think Tía Lola can tell.

"What's the matter, Lola?" she asks, taking my hand.

"Tía Lola," I answer, "how can I go home after seeing palaces and pyramids and llamas? I'll miss my new friends, and most of all, I'll miss you. I don't want to leave Peru."

"You'll be okay, my darling," she says. "Your home is a pretty amazing place, too. Tell me, what do you like best about it?"

"Hmmmm," I say, sniffling. "I like my

dog, Bean. I do miss him. And I like my friends, especially Josh and Bella. And my room. Did you know that it's painted purple with orange polka dots? You should come see it."

"I will someday," Tía Lola says. "Tell me what else you like about home."

"Well, I do like my school, Northland Elementary," I say, thinking out loud. "My teacher, Ms. Garcia, is pretty awesome… and the Orange Smoothies! I love my soccer team."

"There you go," says Tía Lola. "Your home is full of so many wonderful things, including your family," she says.

"But what about you?" I ask.

"I'm there, too, Lola."

"You are?" I say. "Do you mean you are going to visit us soon?"

"I am going to try to visit more often," Tía Lola says, "but that's not what I'm talking about right now."

"I don't understand," I say. "How will you be with me at home?"

"I'll be with you here and here," she says, pointing to my head and my heart. "And I'll always be at the other end of the phone or a letter, too. Okay?"

"Okay!" I say, and hug her tight.

We make it to the airport on time—barely. On the way there, Ben realizes that he left Lorenzo the stuffed llama at Tía Lola's house. He gets so upset that Tía Lola turns around and goes back to the house. I can tell that Mom and Dad don't think that's a good idea, but Tía Lola says, "I don't want my Benito's last memory of Peru to be a sad one!" She gets us home, finds the llama under Ben's bed, and then manages to get us to the airport just in time to catch the plane. We are all running so fast that we don't have too much time to be sad, so that's good.

When we get to our seats on the plane, huffing, puffing, and sweating, I tell the flight attendant, "We Levines are very dramatic." And she just smiles.

"Want to kiss Lorenzo the llama?" Ben asks her.

"Can I give him a hug instead?" she says, and Ben agrees.

Chapter Seven
Home

Dear *Diario,*

It's my first night home, and my whole vacation seems like a dream. Was I really just in Peru with

Tía Lola and my family and all my new friends at San Martín? I know I was. I can't wait to tell Bella and Josh all about my trip and share my reports with my second grade class. I think everyone will like the presents I brought them!

Shalom,
Lola Levine

P.S. I hope I dream of Peru.

A week later, on the first Sunday morning after my trip, I wake up with my dog curled at the foot of my bed.

"Good morning, Bean!" I say, and reach over to put him in my lap. I can use a long

puppy cuddle. I miss Tía Lola. Then I notice there is a note on Mia's goldfish bowl.

"Breakfast surprise at 8 o'clock!" it says. "The usual place."

I know that Mom and Dad aren't going to surprise us with another trip to Peru, so I wonder what the surprise is.

Mom is making banana smoothies and Dad is toasting bagels.

"Yum!" I say. "Did you get the bagels from Biff's Bagels?"

"Yep!" says Dad. "And that's not all. I went to a new grocery store and look what I found!"

On the table there is a big bowl of delicious mangos that glow yellow, orange, and red. I read the sticker on one of them and it says GROWN IN PERU.

"Yay!" I say. "I can't believe it!" I smell the delicious mango, and I am back in Tía Lola's kitchen, even if it's just in my imagination.

Thwunk! I hear Ben jumping down the last three stairs as usual. But this time there's also another *Thwunk! Kerplunk!* and an "Ouch!" Ben hops in.

"I stubbed my toe!" he says. "Ouch. Double ouch!"

"Uh-oh," Mom says. "Are you okay?"

"I am now!" he says, plopping down at the table. "Biff's bagels! Yum!"

A couple of weeks later, we get a big envelope all the way from Peru. It's from Tía Lola! She has letters for each of us—and pictures, too. I

put mine up on my dresser in my bedroom
to look at every morning and night. Instead
of making me sad, it makes me smile.

Dear Tía Lola,

How are you? Thank you for the
pictures! They are great. Please
say hi to my friends at San Martín,

especially Lucia and Lucas! I'm including these notes for them and also these two Orange Smoothie soccer shirts. Dad is the coach, and he let me order two extra! I gave my reports at school, and everyone was amazed. They can't believe that I got to climb the Temple of the Sun and pet a llama. I think they wished they could go to Peru, too. I really miss you but keep remembering what you told me just before we left: that I carry you—and Peru—in my heart.

I'm sending you lots of *besos* and *abrazos*, kisses and hugs.

Shalom,
Lola Levine

Don't miss
Lola's next adventure!

Available JULY 2017

Dear *Diario,*

Yay! It's almost Halloween! And since Halloween is on a Sunday this year, it's going to be a Halloweekend! I am so excited. Halloween is one of my favorite holidays, and not just because I love witches and ghosts and monsters, but also because I love candy! And I really don't get to eat a lot of candy, except for Halloween. My parents don't let me. Mom says that candy doesn't help build strong bodies. When we want something sweet, she sometimes suggests raisins, which she says are "nature's candy."

About two days after Halloween, Mom always has the idea that we should trade what's left of our candy for something else, like a new book or toy. It's her idea, not ours, but it seems like we always end up agreeing to Mom's ideas. I'm getting sleepy now, so...

Shalom and good night,
Lola Levine

Chapter One
Boo!

On Monday morning, I wake up extra early because I have a plan. My plan is to scare my little brother, Ben. He's okay most of the time, but he also bugs me. He likes to make jokes, and sometimes they are about me.

Last week, he kept saying "Dolores is a brontosaurus! Dolores is a brontosaurus!" because he likes rhymes. Dolores is my first name, but I go by Lola.

"I'm NOT a brontosaurus!" I tell Ben. "Dinosaurs have small brains, and mine is big!"

Ben might be good at rhyming, but guess what? I'm good at scaring people, and since it's almost Halloween, I'm going to scare Ben this morning. I wait outside his door until I hear my dad call up the stairs like he does every morning before school.

"Kids! Wake up! Breakfast in fifteen minutes!"

I hear some mumbles and grumbles,

and then I hear Ben get up. I know he'll come out of his room soon, so I pretend to be a ghost and throw on a white sheet with holes cut out for the eyes. I crouch and wait, and when Ben steps into the hallway, I jump out in front of him and say, "Boo!" Ben jumps back and trips over his own feet. "Gotcha!" I say, and start laughing.

Ben does not think this is as funny as I do.

"You scared me, Lola! And it's not even Halloween yet," he complains.

"Well, it's Halloweek," I say, and pat him on the head. Then I go back to my room to get ready for school.

"I'll get you back!" Ben says.

"I hope so!" I say. I like surprises.

Dad makes us pumpkin pancakes for

breakfast. Not only do they have pumpkin flavor, but they are shaped like pumpkins, too! It's going to be a great day.

When I get to school, I run over to Josh Blot and Bella Benitez, my super best friends.

"What are you going to be for Halloween?" I ask.

"I'm going to be a firefighter," says Josh.

"That's awesome," I say. "How about you, Bella?"

"I'm going to be a fairy," she says.

"How cool!" I say. "You'll be a great fairy. When you dance ballet, it sometimes looks like you are flying." Bella loves to dance.

"How about you?" Bella asks.

"I'm not sure yet," I say. "I might be a zombie—or a vampire. It has to be something really scary. We always make our costumes, because my dad believes in 'creative expression,' but we did buy lots of black and white makeup and fake blood at the store this weekend."

Alyssa Goldstein and Makayla Miller must be listening, because all of a sudden Alyssa says, "Gross. I don't know why you'd want to wear fake blood or look like a monster."

"I happen to like monsters," I say back. "What are you going to be for Halloween?"

"Princesses," Alyssa and Makayla say at the same time. Somehow, I'm not surprised. They sometimes act like they rule the school, but they really don't. They like to tease me and other people, too. The bell rings, and we all walk into Ms. Garcia's second-grade classroom and sit down.

"Good morning, students!" Ms. Garcia says.

"Good morning, Ms. Garcia!" we answer back.

"Is everyone excited for the Fall Festival?" Ms. Garcia asks.

"Yes!" the whole class says at once.

"We are going to have so many fun events this week," Ms. Garcia says. "There are lots of celebrations during the fall, all over the world. For example, Chinese people celebrate the Moon Festival in mid-autumn. They gather with friends and family for parades under the moonlight, carrying lanterns and dancing. They celebrate, give thanks, and eat mooncakes.

"Mexicans and Mexican Americans like me celebrate Dia de los Muertos, the Day of the Dead, at the start of November. We create altars for our loved ones who have passed. Many in the United States celebrate Halloween."

"We celebrate Dia de los Muertos, too!" says Bella.

"That's wonderful!" says Ms. Garcia. "Fall is an important time of year for many people. Here at Northland Elementary we will have the Fall Festival this week to celebrate the transition of summer into winter during the season of autumn."

"I know a girl named Autumn!" says Juan Gomez. "She lives on my block."

"That's a nice name," says Ms. Garcia. "What do we know about autumn, the season also called fall?" I raise my hand, and Ms. Garcia calls on me.

"It's the time of year when trees' leaves change color and then fall off," I say.

"That's right, Lola," says Ms. Garcia. "We have four seasons: summer, fall, winter, and spring. We call trees that lose all their leaves seasonally deciduous trees." Then she writes the word *deciduous* on the board. It sounds like dee-sid-you-us. "Autumn is also the time when some of the food we eat is harvested, including apples."

"Yum!" I say. "Do we get to visit an apple orchard, Ms. Garcia? Because I know last year's second graders did."

"Yes, we do," says Ms. Garcia. "On

Wednesday, we will go to Feliz Manzana Farm and pick some apples. Can anyone tell me what *feliz manzana* means in English?" I raise my hand, but Bella is quicker. "What does it mean, Bella?"

"It means 'happy apple,'" Bella says with a smile.

"I speak Spanish, too," I say.

"We all know that," says Makayla, rolling her eyes. I roll mine back.

"Tomorrow, we'll collect leaves and decorate the classroom with leaf art. We'll visit the farm on Wednesday, and Thursday is Pumpkin Day! Each of you will bring a pumpkin to school. We'll weigh, measure, and describe the pumpkins. After that, you'll get to paint them. And then, finally, we are going to have a school parade on Friday during lunchtime recess. Each of you will get to dress as one of your favorite characters from a book or from history."

I already know who my favorite book character is. I'm going to dress up as Marisol McDonald from my favorite picture book, *Marisol McDonald Doesn't Match.* Marisol is bilingual, just like me. She likes to mismatch on purpose. Best of all, she's always true to herself, even if it means people tease her sometimes.

"Hooray! Hooray! Pumpkin Day!" I say, and everyone laughs. It feels nice— not like they are laughing at me, but like they are laughing with me.